First Experiences

Katie goes to the Hospital

Written by **Barbara Taylor Cork**

Illustrated by **Siobhan Dodds**

BRIMAX

This is Katie. She is looking after her teddy. He has a bad earache. Katie often gets earache too. Tomorrow she is going to hospital to have an operation on her ear.

Mother is going to stay with Katie in the hospital. Katie helps Mother pack their case. "Teddy wants to come too," says Katie. "That's fine," says Mother.

The next morning, Katie feels a bit worried.
She is pleased that Mother is going with her.
Katie doesn't have any breakfast, because she must
not eat or drink anything before the operation.

Father is staying at home to look after Katie's baby sister, Sarah. "We'll come and see you tomorrow," he says, waving goodbye.

Katie holds Mother's hand as they walk down a long corridor to the Rainbow Ward.
"Hospitals smell funny," says Katie.
"That's the smell of the medicines they use to make people better," says Mother.

When they get to the Rainbow Ward a nurse greets them. "Hello Katie," says the nurse. "Let me show you to your bed."

"Look, there's your name," says Mother. The bed has sides, so that Katie won't fall out. There is a chart at the end of the bed to keep a record of Katie's temperature and pulse.

"You can put your things in this cupboard," says the nurse, helping Katie to unpack.
A little boy called Peter comes over to meet Katie. "Yesterday, Peter had the same operation as you're going to have," says the nurse. "He's much better now."

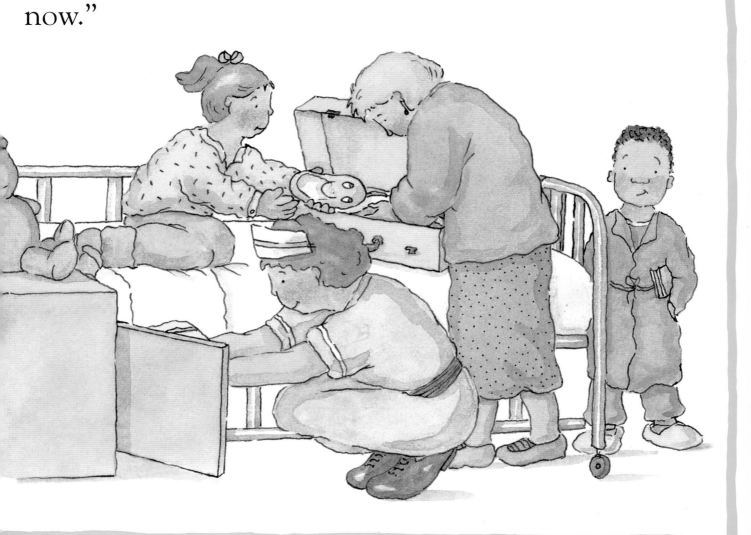

The nurse puts a name bracelet on Katie's wrist.
This shows the doctors and nurses who she is.
"Can my teddy have one too?" asks Katie.
"Of course he can," says the nurse, with a smile.

"Come along Katie," says the nurse. "We need to take your temperature and check your pulse."

The nurse then uses a special machine to check Katie's blood pressure. She writes down the results on Katie's chart.

The doctor arrives and tells Katie and Mother about the operation. Then she looks in Katie's ears.

"Now I need to listen to your chest with this," she says, putting her stethoscope on Katie's skin. "Ooh, that tickles," laughs Katie.

While the other children in the ward are eating their lunch, Mother takes Katie to have a bath. Teddy comes to watch.

When Katie is washed and dried, Mother dresses her in a special gown for the operation.
"Stand still while I tie it at the back," says Mother.
Katie also has to wear a hat to keep her hair tidy.

Soon it will be time for Katie's operation. The nurse gives her some medicine. "In a little while," says the nurse, "you will feel sleepy and your mouth might feel a bit dry."

A porter lifts Katie onto a trolley and wheels her to the operating room. Mother, teddy, and the nurse go with her.

"Hello Katie," says a doctor. "I'm going to look after you while you have your operation. You will feel a little scratch on your hand and soon you will be fast asleep. When you wake up, it will all be over."

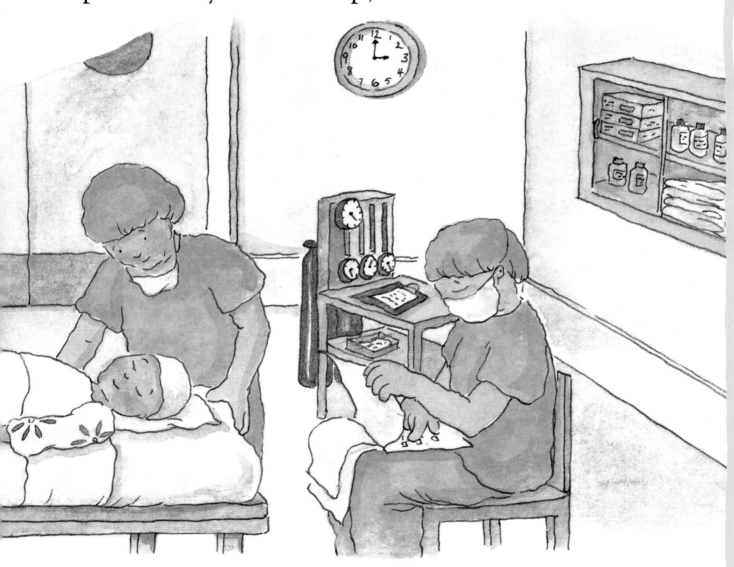

In the operating room, the doctors and nurses wear special clothes and masks to keep the room clean. They even wear hats like the one Katie is wearing.

When the operation is over, the porter wheels Katie back to Rainbow Ward. She is still very sleepy. Mother sits beside her and holds her hand. The nurse checks to make sure Katie is alright.

Katie wakes up and sees her mother. For a little while she feels a bit sick and her ear is sore. The nurse gives Katie a drink of water because she is very thirsty.

Katie sleeps well all night. Mother stays in the hospital too, and sleeps in a bed beside her.

The next day, Katie feels much better. Father and baby Sarah come to see her. They bring her a present and a card. "As soon as the doctor has seen you, you can come home," says Father.

Mother packs their case and helps Katie to get dressed. Katie says goodbye to Peter and the other children in the ward. "Thank you for all your help," says Mother to the doctor and nurse.

Katie is very happy to be home again. Her room looks just the same. "It's nice to have you back," says Father, and gives her a big hug.